JP
BRI

Brisson, Pat

Benny's pennies.

$14.95

BENNY'S PENNIES

A DOUBLEDAY BOOK FOR YOUNG READERS

BENNY'S PENNIES

BY PAT BRISSON · ILLUSTRATED BY BOB BARNER

For my very own Benjamin Thomas Brisson.
With love, Mombo
P.B.

For Luddie

B.B.

A Doubleday Book for Young Readers
PUBLISHED BY DELACORTE PRESS
Bantam Doubleday Dell Publishing Group, Inc.
1540 Broadway, New York, New York 10036
DOUBLEDAY and the portrayal of an anchor with a dolphin are
trademarks of Bantam Doubleday Dell Publishing Group, Inc.
Text copyright © 1993 by Pat Brisson
Illustrations copyright © 1993 by Bob Barner

Library of Congress Cataloging in Publication Data
Brisson, Pat.
Benny's pennies / by Pat Brisson; illustrated by Bob Barner.
— 1st ed.
          p.   cm.
Summary: Benny sets off in the morning with five shiny
new pennies to spend and eventually buys something for his
mother, brother, sister, dog, and cat.
ISBN 0-385-41602-4
[1. Money — Fiction. 2. Counting.] I. Barner, Bob, ill.
II. Title.
PZ7.B78046Be   1993
[E] — dc20   90-21799   CIP   AC

RL: 2.2
Manufactured in Hong Kong
September 1993
10 9 8 7 6 5 4 3 2 1

The illustrations for this book were
created with torn and cut papers from
Mexico, France, Japan, India, and the
United States, pastels, colored pen-
cils, various types of glue and paints.
The text is set in 18 point Benguiat
Book. Typography by Lynn Braswell.

Benny McBride had five new pennies.
"What should I buy?" he asked.

"Buy something beautiful," said his mom.
"Buy something good to eat," said his brother.

"Buy something nice to wear," said his sister.
"Woof! Woof!" said his dog.
"Meow!" said his cat.

"OK," Benny said. "I will."
So Benny McBride, with five new
pennies, strolled out in the morning sun.

A woman was cutting roses. Her name was Mrs. Hill.

"Will you sell me a rose?" asked Benny.
"Will you sell me a rose for a penny?"
"Yes, I will," said Mrs. Hill.

Then Benny McBride, with four new pennies and a sweet-smelling rose, strolled on in the morning sun.

A girl was baking cookies.
Her name was Lucy May.

"Will you sell me a cookie?" asked Benny.
"Will you sell me a cookie for a penny?"
"A cookie for a penny? OK," said Lucy May.

Then Benny McBride, with three new pennies,
a sweet-smelling rose, and a soft warm
cookie, strolled on in the morning sun.

A boy was making hats.
His name was Michael Bess.

"Will you sell me a hat?" asked Benny.
"Will you sell me a hat for a penny?"
"Yes, oh yes," said Michael Bess.

Then Benny McBride, with two new pennies, a sweet-smelling rose, a soft warm cookie, and a fine paper hat, strolled on in the morning sun.

A butcher was cutting meat. His name was Mr. Hopper.

"Will you sell me a bone?" asked Benny.
"Will you sell me a bone for a penny?"
"You're quite a shopper," said Mr. Hopper.

Then Benny McBride, with one new penny, a sweet-smelling rose, a soft warm cookie, a fine paper hat, and a big meaty bone, strolled on in the morning sun.

A man was catching fish. His name was Mr. Beal.

"Will you sell me a fish?" asked Benny.
"Will you sell me a fish for a penny?"
"It's a deal," said Mr. Beal.

Then Benny McBride, with a sweet-
smelling rose, a soft warm cookie, a fine
paper hat, a big meaty bone, a floppy
wet fish — but no new pennies — strolled
home in the morning sun.

"I'm back!" he called. "And I bought
what you said."

"It's beautiful!" said his mom.
"Mmm, good!" said his brother.
"I like it!" said his sister.
"Woof! Woof!" said his dog.
"Meow!" said his cat.

"Thank you, Benny!" they all said together.
"You're welcome," said Benny McBride.